# Cookie meets Peanut

*Cookie Meets Peanut* is dedicated to my little "peanut," Bryn, and her furry big sister, who have filled my heart with love and my life with laughter. My incredible memories with my beautiful baby girl and my fourteen-year-old beloved dog make everything else in life seem so small and inconsequential. To all the mommies who have furry babies and real babies, read and enjoy this book with your loved ones.

XO,

To Laura: You're my cookie, peanut, and whole enchilada.
—DR

## ABOUT THIS BOOK

The illustrations for this book were created digitally with
Corel software and hand drawn with the Intuos4 Wacom tablet.
The text was set in Baskerville, and the display type is
hand lettered by the illustrator. This book was edited by
Erin Stein and designed by Patti Ann Harris. The production was
supervised by Erika Schwartz, and the production editor was Andy Ball.

Text and artwork copyright © 2014 by Big Talk LLC • Jacket art by Daniel Roode • Cover design by Patti Ann Harris • Cover copyright © 2014 Hachette Book Group, Inc. • All rights reserved. In accordance with the U.S. Copyright Act of 1976, the scanning, uploading, and electronic sharing of any part of this book without the permission of the publisher is unlawful piracy and theft of the author's intellectual property. If you would like to use material from the book (other than for review purposes), prior written permission must be obtained by contacting the publisher at permissions@hbgusa.com. Thank you for your support of the author's rights. • Little, Brown and Company • Hachette Book Group • 237 Park Avenue, New York, NY 10017 • Visit our website at lb-kids.com • Little, Brown and Company is a division of Hachette Book Group, Inc. • The Little, Brown name and logo are trademarks of Hachette Book Group, Inc. • The publisher is not responsible for websites (or their content) that are not owned by the publisher. • First Edition: September 2014 • Library of Congress Cataloging-in-Publication Data • Frankel, Bethenny, 1970– • Cookie meets Peanut / written by Bethenny Frankel ; illustrated by Daniel Roode. — First edition. • pages cm • Summary: Cookie the dog enjoys all of Mommy's attention until baby Peanut arrives. • ISBN 978-0-316-36843-8 (hardcover)—ISBN 978-0-316-36844-5 (ebook) [1. Dogs—Fiction. 2. Babies—Fiction.] I. Roode, Daniel, illustrator. II. Title. • PZ7.F8532Coo 2014 • [E]—dc23 • 2014004120 • 10 9 8 7 6 5 4 3 2 1 • WOR • Printed in the United States of America

# Cookie meets Peanut

## by bethenny frankel

illustrated by
## daniel roode

**L B**

Little, Brown
New York • Boston

Cookie and Mommy live in the big city, full of skyscrapers, shops, and bustling busy people. Every morning, Mommy wakes up to hear...

WOOF! WOOF!

SCRITCH! SCRATCH! SCRITCH!

It's Cookie, saying it's time to go!
"Okay, BooBoo! I'm coming," says Mommy.

Cookie is Mommy's Furry Baby.
Mommy loves how Cookie's nose
looks like a little piece of black licorice.
Every day, Cookie and Mommy
go on walksies.

Every day, Cookie barks

WOOF! at the doorman,

WOOF! at the neighbor, and

WOOF! at the policeman.

BARK JAC

Mommy gets a coffee at Starbarks
while Cookie sneaks a bite of bagel.
They window-shop at Bark Jacobs.

Cookie runs into the store and comes out with a shoe.
"Cookie! That's cute!" Mommy says.

Mommy and Cookie spend every day together.
Until, one morning, Mommy leaves without taking Cookie for walksies.
And when she comes home, Mommy has someone new with her.

"Cookie, meet Peanut. Isn't she the cutest baby in the world?"
Cookie goes to her hiding spot. *She* is Mommy's Furry Baby.
She has no interest in this new Peanut.
*WOOF! WOOF!*
"That's not nice, Cookie. You stay out of Peanut's room
until you can be a nice girl."

Pretty soon, Peanut starts to crawl
out of her room.
Peanut follows Cookie,
crawling on her tiny hands and legs.

WOOF!
WOOF!

Pretty soon, Peanut starts to talk.

"Coo Coo!" says Peanut, trying to say Cookie's name.

Cookie barks and goes back under the sofa. *WOOF! WOOF!*

Soon, Peanut can walk *and* talk.
Now, every day, Mommy takes Peanut for walksies.
Cookie wants to go, too!
"No, Cookie!" cries Peanut. "Just Mommy and me!"
"Be nice to Cooks," says Mommy.
"Bye, Cookie. We'll be home soon."

Cookie misses barking at the doorman, at the neighbor, and at the policeman.
She misses going to Starbarks and Bark Jacobs. She misses having a bite of bagel.
She misses Mommy.

Cookie and Peanut are not the same.
Peanut loves a dance party.
She loves to whirl and twirl.

Cookie will not dance.
She sits down and shakes her tail.

WOOF! WOOF!

Cookie and Peanut do not eat the same.
Peanut cleans her plate without dropping
one pea on the floor.

Cookie flings crumbs everywhere
and then looks around for more.

Peanut loves to play princess and dress up
in tutus and tiaras.
She loves pink, polka dots, and sparkles.
She loves rainbows, ribbons, and lollipops.

Cookie does not like any of those things!
She will not wear a tutu or a tiara.
Cookie does not like pink, polka dots, or sparkles!
Cookie's black nose twitches. It does look like fun.
She might like to lick a lollipop....

Peanut wants to play dress-up in Mommy's closet,
but she has no one to play with.
"Cookie, please play with me?" she asks.
Cookie follows Peanut but tries to hide in a corner.

Peanut plops a hat on Cookie's head. "Pretty!" she says.
WOOF! WOOF! barks Cookie, shaking off the hat.

"Don't be grouchy, Cookie!" says Mommy.
"Here—you two play in Peanut's room while
I'm cooking in the kitchen.
I put some berries out for a snack."

"Let's make a present for Mommy," says Peanut.
"We will make Sparkle Tea with glitter
and BooBooBerry Soup."

WOOF!
WOOF!

Peanut pours blue glitter
into a teapot and adds her juice.
Cookie helps stir.

Using her hat as a bowl,
Peanut pours in berries and
more juice, plus a pinch of cocoa!
Cookie barks.
*WOOF! WOOF!*
"Good idea," says Peanut. She mashes
the berries together and mixes the soup.
Cookie tastes it. *WOOF!* It's good!

Peanut pours Sparkle Tea for herself,
for Mommy, and for Cookie
into three pretty teacups.
Then she sets out three bowls
of BooBooBerry Soup.

"Mommy, come see what Cookie and I made for you!" cries Peanut.

WOOF!
WOOF!
WOOF!

"Thank you," says Mommy.
"It's so nice to see you playing together, just like sisters!"
Cookie nudges Peanut's hand with her wet licorice nose
and wags her scruffy tail.
Peanut giggles. "She's my furry sister."

Every day Mommy, Peanut, and Cookie go for walksies.

Cookie barks *WOOF!* at the doorman,

*WOOF!* at the neighbor, and

*WOOF!* at the policeman while Peanut waves to them.

Mommy gets a coffee at Starbarks, and they window-shop at Bark Jacobs.

Each night they snuggle
in a big pile together.
"Mommy, I love you."
"I love you, too, Peanut."
"I love Cookie, too."
"Me, too. She's your
furry big sister."
Cookie says good night.
*WOOF! WOOF!*